AF584330

SECRETS OF THE SEASONS

Heidi Cooper Smith

Windy Hollow Books

Scorching days burn long and bright,
and shriveled grasses crunch.

Gusts of dust brush our skin.

Swaying and sighing, we prickle and wilt.

High in treetops, cicadas drone.

With sweating hands, we cover our ears
as they buzz inside our heads.

Throbbing and quivering,
they rasp and shriek.

Dark clouds rumble and tumble,
as lightning cracks the sky.

Rain arrives in a thundering rush
and the air fills with fresh new smells.

*Slipping and sliding,
we splosh and squelch.*

We search the pools
and puddles for frogs.

When we lunge, they skip away
and disappear from sight.

Peeping and pulsing,
they chirp and trill.

Too soon, the days grow shorter.
Leaves stiffen and drift on the breeze.

They gather in piles, calling our names.

Kicking and skidding,
we spin and leap.

An early frost bites
the grass, and shines
in the morning sun.

Fruit bats gather
and huddle in clumps.

*Squealing and squabbling,
they cackle and screech.*

Mornings creep in, dark and late,
through a window white with fog.

Smoke from the wood stove
tickles our noses.

*Stretching and shivering,
we snuggle and snooze.*

Slimy snails seal their shells.

Lacy spirals pile in tight —
clinging close, out of sight.

Slinking and sliding,
they nestle and ooze.

Everything slows as the earth settles…

In time the cold begins to ease;
the days stretch out again.

New growth shoots in shades of green.
The ground begins to stir.

Flowers bloom
and bees bustle.

*Bobbing
and hovering,
they murmur
and hum.*

Birds flood the trees
and carol till we wake.

The gentle sun calls us to play
and the air fills with movement
and life.

Tingling and giggling,
we chase and shout.

Wary magpies watch and wait.
Without warning, they swoop.

Our hearts race as they duck and dive.

Warbling and gargling, they jabber and squawk.

Dusk lingers long
into the night,
and crickets creak till dawn.

We gaze from our window
in wonder and long
for the world to awake.

Skipping
and dancing,

we cheer and sing.

For Mum and Dad and Wendy, with love.

After spending 20 years playing with clay for a living, Heidi suddenly found herself with three children under four, so she joined an online illustration challenge during nap time to stay sane. Six months later she was offered her first illustration contract and began writing soon after. She was lucky enough to grow up on a large property near Girraween National Park and the memories from this magical childhood provided the inspiration for this book.

First published in hardback in 2022
by Windy Hollow Books

PO Box 265, Kew East, Victoria, Australia 3102
www.windyhollowbooks.com.au
www.facebook.com/windyhollowbooks

Text and Illustration copyright © Heidi Cooper Smith 2022
The moral rights of the author and illustrator
have been asserted.

This book is copyright. Apart from any fair dealing for the purposes of private study, research, criticism or review permitted under the Copyright Act 1968, no part may be stored or reproduced by any process without prior written permission. Enquiries should be made to the publisher.

ISBN: 9780645323542 (hardback)
Design by Nuovo Group

A catalogue record for this book is available from the National Library of Australia